# HOLY SPIRIT
# ME TOO!

# Holy Spirit Me, Too!

XULON PRESS

Xulon Press
2301 Lucien Way #415
Maitland, FL 32751
407.339.4217
www.xulonpress.com

Unless otherwise indicated, Scripture quotations taken from the King James Version (KJV)–*public domain.*

ISBN-13: 978-1-6628-3128-7
ISBN-13: 978-1-6628-3129-4

This book is dedicated to my family:
The Father, Jesus, and the Holy Spirit.

But Jesus said, "Let the children come to me. Don't stop them! For the Kingdom of Heaven belongs to those who are like these children." (Matthew 19:14)

# Table of Contents

# Chapter 1

# Home Sweet Home

Daddy is an architect. He draws buildings and houses on paper from high up on his chair and big drawing table. He drew our house too. Our house is a country cottage with lots of rooms.

*And my people shall dwell in a peaceable habitation, and in sure dwellings, and in quiet resting places.* (Isaiah 32:18)

We have a sunroom with many green plants. I help Mommy take care of them. Sometimes, we have tea parties in it. We use the prettiest plates and tea cups. It is a special place for us to be together.

Mommy put colorful, flower wallpaper in different rooms.

"Victorian beauty," she said.

One morning, Daddy and I walked from room to room. We looked at the different kinds of wood everywhere. Each one had a pretty color. We saw lots of lines and circles in them.

Daddy said there are two kinds of wood - hardwoods and softwoods. Hardwoods have flowers and make seeds. Softwoods make cones. I learned the names of the different woods built into my house. There is cherry, mahogany, oak, teak, walnut, cedar, and pine. Each is a living beauty! I like to sit on the wooden floors when I play with my toys. My chariots slide easily across them.

*I am more than a conqueror!* (Romans 8:37)

*And he answered, "Fear not: for they that be with us are more than they that be with them." And Elisha prayed, and said, "Lord, I pray thee, open his eyes, that he may see." And the Lord opened the eyes of the young man; and he saw: behold, the mountain was full of horses and chariots of fire round about Elisha.* (2 Kings 6:16-17)

Daddy likes to show me pictures of trees from different books. There are so many kinds of trees that live in so many different places. Daddy said trees give us shelter from the wind, snow, and rain. They even clean the air we breathe! Trees are so nice to us. They help us. They keep us warm from the winter cold. I remember to say "thank you" to them when I play outside.

*Let the field be joyful, and all that is therein: then shall all the trees of the wood rejoice before the*

*Lord for he cometh, for he cometh to judge the earth: he shall judge the world with righteousness and the people with his truth.* (Psalms 96:12-13)

We have warm fireplaces too. Daddy drew them on paper first before they were made. In the winter, we snuggle together in front of them. We read and drink lots of hot chocolate, with marshmallows on top. Mommy and Daddy love to hold me in their arms. I do so love to be in their warm arms too. I feel safe and secure. My body becomes as still as a Blue Heron standing in the water. My thoughts slow down like a train about to stop at its next station. Little by little, I fall asleep.

*And he shall turn the heart of the fathers to the children, and the heart of the children to their fathers, lest I come and smite the earth with a curse.* (Malachi 4:6)

Roses cover the sides of our cottage outside. I like to look at how they climb up and go sideways. I watch them grow taller and wider each day. They smell nice. We have flowers, butterflies, birds, and bees around the outside of our house. They visit us and some live in our garden.

*And the Lord said, I have surely seen the affliction of my people which are in Egypt, and have heard their cry by reason of their taskmasters; for I know their sorrows; And I am come down to deliver them out of the hand of the Egyptians, and to bring them up out of that land unto a good land and a large, unto a land flowing with milk and honey;* (Exodus 3:7-8)

Daddy is a beekeeper. It is his hobby. It makes him happy. The bees give us lots of honey. Daddy taught me many wonderful things about how the bees and their beehives work. We wear funny suits in case the bees get excited and try to sting us.

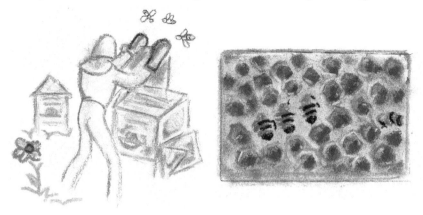

Daddy helped me to understand how very important the honeybee is for us today. He said, "The honeybee is a special flying insect sent from God. It gives us delicious honey. It visits the vegetables, fruits and nuts to help them give us more food too." I do like to eat honey with peaches and cream. Would you like to eat some too?

One morning, as Daddy was putting some of the honeybees' honey in a glass jar, we studied its honeycomb. He said, "Look at this magnificent piece of engineering and planning! The design of this hexagonal honeycomb is exceptional. It shows mathematics at its best. In geometry, my little wonder, a hexagon can be defined as a polygon with six sides. This two-dimensional shape has 6 sides, 6 vertices and 6 angles. A polygon is a plane figure with at least 3 straight sides and angles."

Daddy knew I did not understand what he told me at that moment. As soon as we returned to the house he made a hexagon out of construction paper showing me its sides. I could see the sides and angles of the polygon too. It was then I understood what he said at the bee hive. The new vocabulary words came alive right in front of my eyes. Math is fun, especially when

Daddy is my teacher. I began to see polygons and hexagons everywhere. Everything has math in it! Even a Nautilus shell has math hidden inside of it. Look inside one and you will see.

Daddy said, "Look at this cutaway of one and see how the chambers are arranged in an approximately logarithmic spiral having equal ratios with equal distances apart."

I didn't understand at first what Daddy told me until he showed me what a cutaway was in the Nautilus shell. The top part of the shell was missing. You then get to look inside. The chambers in it were like rooms. Each was perfectly made for the other working together so the Nautilus could swim. I ran to Mommy later and shared these new vocabulary words with her. She especially liked the "logarithmic spiral" word even though I pronounced it funny. She smiled when I told her what it meant.

Learning is fun and full of surprises. I was told that the bees even use the beeswax that is made from their own bodies to make their honeycombs. I couldn't do that!

I tasted some honey Daddy gave me at the hive and it was so sweet and gooey. "Honey is one of our perfect foods, God's gift to us. The bees make enough for them and even some for us too." Daddy smiled as he spoke these words to me. God is so kind to give us honey. I am thankful! Aren't you?

> *The fear of the Lord is clean, enduring forever:*
> *the judgments of the Lord are true and righteous*
> *altogether. More to be desired are they than gold:*
> *sweeter also than honey and the honeycomb.*
> (Psalms 19:9-10)

# Chapter 2

# Heavenly Birth

When I drew a picture of our house, I showed it to Daddy and asked him, "Does Jesus have a house like we do? Daddy, where is Jesus's house? Where does Jesus live?"

Daddy answered, "Jesus's house is in my heart. He lives in Daddy's heart. It is a grand house!" Wow! I looked at Daddy and saw a great, big house sitting in his heart.

I asked, "Is Mommy's heart Jesus's house too?"

Daddy replied, "Yes, Jesus lives in Mommy's heart too."

"Daddy," I said, "I want Jesus to make His house in my heart just like you and Mommy. Will Jesus come to live in my heart too?"

Daddy smiled and said, "Yes, He will! Just ask Him."

"Jesus," I whispered. "Here is Your new house, my heart. Please come and live in my heart just like Mommy and Daddy. Thank you, Jesus. I hope You will like Your new house."

I asked Daddy why Jesus had so many houses. He told me Jesus wanted to live inside the hearts of many families just like ours, even though each one was different and may live far away. It made Him happy.

*For with the heart man believeth unto righteousness; and with the mouth confession is made unto salvation.* (Romans 10:10)

*God that made the world and all things therein,*
*seeing that he is Lord of heaven and earth dwells*
*not in temples made with hands.* (Acts 17:24)

Daddy and Mommy both said, "Today is a special day for you, just like a birthday!" We celebrated and had a wonderful tea party in our sunroom. Mommy made my favorite cookies, ginger snaps. Daddy brought fresh honey from our bee hives. I did feel special.

*Jesus answered, Verily, verily, I say unto thee, except a man be born again, he cannot see the kingdom of God.* (John 3:3)

*And Jesus called a little child unto him, and set him in the midst of them, And said, Verily I say unto you, except ye be converted and become as little children, ye shall not enter into the kingdom of heaven.* (Matthew 18:2-3)

I helped Mommy clean-up. She let me carry the pretty teapot to the kitchen. Mommy was right beside me all the way, in case I needed help. I was careful and happy to hold the teapot. I felt all grownup.

Mommy likes to shop for different kinds of teas and teapots. I do too. Whenever we found a pretty new teapot in a shop, it was like finding a special, new treasure. We studied it, looked at it, turned it upside down, and if we liked it, we bought it. Mommy dresses me as pretty as a teapot when we go shopping for teapots. Would you like to dress like a pretty teapot too?

Did you know blossom teas flower in warm glass teapots? I watch these closely as they change slowly into flowers. "I am a rare blossom ready to flower, even in the winter," Mommy said.

One morning, I heard Daddy talking to Jesus. "Jesus, will You please bless my new project?" Daddy asked, while drawing inside his workroom.

> *Trust in the Lord with all thine heart; and lean not unto thine own understanding. In all thy ways acknowledge him, and he shall direct thy paths.* (Proverbs 3:5-6)

> *I will instruct thee and teach thee in the way which thou shalt go: I will guide thee with mine eye.* (Psalm 32:8)

> *The steps of a good man are ordered by the Lord:*
> *and he delighteth in his way.* (Psalm 37:23)

I like to skip into Daddy's workroom. He always opens his arms to me. I run to him, giggling all the way. I climb up onto his lap. He kisses my head as I look at his drawings.

I like to look at Daddy's work. He is never too busy to show me what he drew. He said his work begins and ends with Jesus, the Master of all architects. Daddy said, "Jesus is the source of all life, and it is through Him that science, math, music, inventions, and creativity come alive."

> *For of him, and through him, and to him, are*
> *all things: to whom be glory forever. Amen.*
> (Romans 11:36)
>
> *I am Alpha and Omega, the beginning and the*
> *ending saith the Lord which is, and which was, and*
> *which is to come, the Almighty.* (Revelation 1:8)

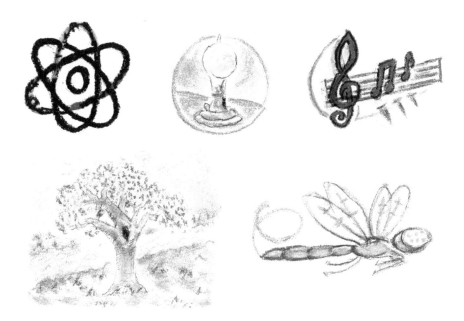

*For by him were all things created, that are in heaven, and that are in earth, visible and invisible, whether they be thrones, or dominions, or principalities, or powers: all things were created by him and for him: And he is before all things, and by him all things consist.* (Colossians 1:16-17)

One afternoon, Daddy pointed to a tree outside the window and said, "Look, my little one, tell me who else could draft such a blueprint as beautiful as a tree?"

I moved my head to agree, having the same mind and heart as Daddy. We looked out the window at the tree together and marveled. "Marveled" is one of our favorite words.

*And he shall be like a tree planted by the rivers of water, that brings forth his fruit in his season; his leaf also shall not wither; and whatsoever he doeth shall prosper.* (Psalms 1:3)

13

*And the multitude of them that believed were of one heart and of one soul: neither said any of them that ought of the things which he possessed was his own; but they all had things in common.* (Acts 4:32)

"Daddy," I asked. "Can I talk to Jesus just like you do?" Daddy answered, "Yes, you can! And He will talk to you."

I believed Daddy. I started to talk to Jesus every day wherever I played.

*Behold, I stand at the door, and knock: if any man hear my voice, and open the door, I will come in to him, and will sup with him, and he with me.* (Revelation 3:20)

# Chapter 3

# Together and Protected

Sometimes at night, Daddy, Mommy and I look through a telescope from our porch. We look at the moon, planets and the stars. Daddy told me that it is our Heavenly Father's good pleasure to give us the kingdom. The earth and all the galaxies, their planets, moons, and stars, near and far, all belonged to us. I was happy, happy to have such gifts. Aren't you happy to have such gifts?

"It is music in orbit, Daddy says, it is the glory of God. He created the heavens and the earth."

> *Fear not, little flock; for it is your Father's good pleasure to give you the kingdom.* (Luke 12:32)
>
> *In the beginning, God created the heavens and the earth.* (Genesis 1:1)
>
> *When the morning stars sang together and all the sons of God shouted for joy.* (Job 38:7)

Mommy taught about the planets and how the stars were born. She said, "You are a star who shines brightly through the night and darkness of this present world."

Do I look like a star? Do I shine very bright in the night? Mommy said I did. I looked through the telescope and believed

I shone just like one of them. I asked, "Mommy, can I dress up like a star tonight?"

> *And they that be wise shall shine as the brightness*
> *of the firmament; and they that turn many to*
> *righteousness as the stars for ever and ever.*
> (Daniel 12:3)

Mommy smiled and laughed at me. I began to yawn, then off we went, as she carried me to my warm bed.

"I love you," Mommy whispered in my ear. I felt her warm kiss on my cheek. "Sleep well, my little one, and do not be afraid, for your Guardian Angels always are here to watch over you. They have been with you since the beginning."

> *The angel of the Lord encampeth round about them*
> *that fear him, and delivereth them.* (Psalms 34:7)

When the weather became warmer, I helped Mommy feed the chickens and collect their eggs. The chickens are so cute and funny. I watch them catch bugs and run in the sun. We let them out of their house early in the morning to walk through the garden. Mommy said this keeps them healthy and happy. I like happy chickens. Before dinner time, they go back into their house for the night, just like we do. Today, I held a chicken gently in my arms. It was so soft and cuddly, I wasn't afraid of it, and it wasn't afraid of me!

Adam and Eve were not afraid of any of the creatures that walked around in their garden in Eden. Daddy read their story to me. They had chickens too. Not one creature harmed another in their beautiful garden. God even brought the creatures to Adam to name them! Daddy said that Adam was the first zoologist. A zoologist is someone who knows about the creatures.

> *And out of the ground the Lord God formed every beast of the field, and every fowl of the air; and brought them unto Adam to see what he would call them: and whatsoever Adam called every living creature, that was the name thereof.* (Genesis 2:19)

# Chapter 4

# Seeds and Stories

We have a garden. It is filled with lots of different vegetables and fruits. We planted them together. What fun we had! There are potatoes, tomatoes, beans, blueberries, raspberries, grapes, strawberries and more. Mommy and I pick the ripe berries and put them in a basket to eat and cook, after we wash them.

> *Blessed shall be thy basket and thy store.*
> (Deuteronomy 28:1-14)

Mommy made yummy berry pies. I helped her put the pie together in the kitchen. I like to learn how to mix and bake! Mommy taught me how to measure with cups and how to hold the parts, to mix together. Sometimes, the flour covers my face and dress. Mommy looks at me and laughs. She said, "You are a true baker, my little Bakester!" I smile and continue to play with the flour.

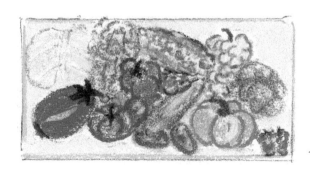

In the spring, we planted the seeds. We ordered seeds and bulbs from seed catalogs that were put in our mailbox in the winter. When they arrived, it made me so happy to look at them. The catalogs were colorful and filled with all kinds of pictures and choices to buy. Seeds and bulbs are amazing! They grow in the earth after being planted, and change into beautiful things.

> *Now the parable is this: The seed is the word of God.* (Matthew 13:3-9;18-23; Luke 8:11)

Before we dug in the soil, Mommy would dress me in my garden work clothes. It is fun to get the soil all over my hands and clothes. I like to work in the garden with Mommy and Daddy. The sun feels warm and my heart feels warm too.

Mommy and Daddy watch me as I work in the garden. They gave me my very own patch of soil to plant. My hands filled with seeds and soil. Did you know that the tiny seeds grow up to become big plants and each one is different? Daddy said that we are made in God's image, but not everyone looks the same on the outside.

> *And God said, let us make man in our own image, after our likeness: and let them have dominion over the fish of the sea, and over the fowl of the air, and over the cattle, and over all the earth, and over every creeping thing that creepeth upon the earth.* (Genesis 1:26)

> *So God created man in his own image, in the image of God created he him; male and female created he them.* (Genesis 1:27)

Mommy said that I am a precious seed that fell on good soil and would grow up a "hundred fold." A hundred fold seemed like a lot to me. I asked her what it meant. She told me that a hundred fold means as 100 times as much. When you have one potato and then you have 100 potatoes from the one potato, then this is an example of a time when the number of potatoes increased a hundred fold. I quickly learned about potatoes and the hundred fold. I believed Mommy. I would grow up like the seed planted in good soil. I want to see lots of plants multiply in my garden. I have a garden in my heart too. I like watching my garden grow. What a great harvest there will be, my plants and me!

*But other fell into good ground and brought forth fruit, some an hundredfold, some sixty fold, some thirty-fold.* (Matthew 13:8)

*Then saith he unto his disciples, The harvest truly is plenteous, but the labourers are few; Pray ye therefore the Lord of the harvest, that he will send forth labourers into his harvest.* (Matthew 9:37-38)

I like to watch Mommy as she draws pictures filled with reds, blues, greens, and purples. I sit right beside her at a table in her art room, and draw with my chalk too.

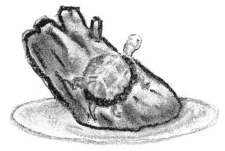

Mommy is writing a new story about turtles. She reads her story to me as she writes it, and the story comes alive. I see the turtles. I hop up and down on my chair and want her to keep reading. I want to know what happens next!

"You have to wait and be patient for the story to be written," Mommy said.

I wrote a little story too! I am just like Mommy. My story is about dragonflies. Mommy showed me pictures of turtles, dragonflies, and other creatures. I drew a blue and yellow dragonfly. Mommy said, "It looks alive and soon will fly off the paper into the garden." I giggled as I watched it fly away.

Mommy believes there were turtles and dragonflies on Noah's Ark. Have you read the story about Noah's Ark? Did your Mommy and Daddy read it to you?

We read the story of Noah's Ark many times. There are many colorful pictures in the book. Lots of creatures were in the ark. Have you ever seen a baby rhinoceros? I like this story because it is true. God saved a family and many different kinds of creatures from the Great Flood.

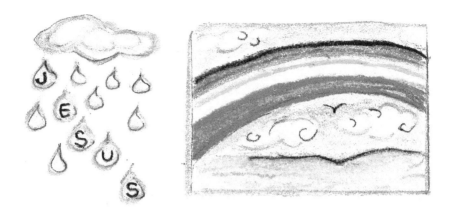

*By faith Noah, being warned of God of things not seen yet, moved with fear, prepared an ark to the saving of his house; by which he condemned the world, and became heir of the righteousness which is by faith.* (Genesis 6:17; Hebrews 11:7)

I asked Mommy many, many questions about the people and the creatures in the ark. I also asked about the rain. I asked her if there would be another flood like that one.

She smiled and said, "No, not like that one, but there will come a flood of His glory upon the whole earth."

I smiled and imagined His glory falling to earth like giant raindrops. Together we drew beautiful, colorful rainbows. Rainbows remind God of His promise to us.

*For the earth shall be filled with the knowledge of the glory of the Lord, as the waters cover the sea.* (Habakkuk 2:14)

*I do set my bow in the cloud, and it shall be for a token of a covenant between me and the earth... never again will the waters become a flood to destroy all life...*(Genesis 9:13-17)

# Chapter 5

# Holy Spirit, Me Too!

One sunny afternoon, Mommy and I walked along the walkway of our pretty flower garden behind the house. She held my hand gently as we walked. We stopped along the way to look closely at some of the flowers' shapes and colors. We watched the bees and butterflies enjoy them too. The birds flew by with songs and calls. I listened to them all. They tweeted so sweet. Did you know they sing to God? I know, Mommy told me so.

> *The flowers appear on the earth; the time of the singing of birds is come, and the voice of the turtle is heard in our land.* (Song of Solomon 2:12)

Mommy began to sing beautiful songs in languages I did not understand. She let go of my hand and started to dance. Mommy's long dress and hair danced with the wind as she twirled and moved. The sun lit up her face. She sang songs with her arms raised high up to Heaven.

> *O sing unto the Lord a new song: sing unto the Lord, all the earth.* (Psalms 96:1)

> *Let them praise his name in the dance: let them sing praises unto him with the timbrel and harp.* (Psalms 149:3)

*And David danced before the Lord with all his*
*might;...and saw king David leaping and dancing*
*before the Lord.* (2 Samuel 6:14,16)

I asked, "Mommy, are these new songs? I don't understand them. Why are you dancing and singing ?"

Mommy did not answer me, and kept singing and dancing. I ran close beside her and tugged at her dress. I jumped up and down. "Mommy, tell me!"

*For he that speaketh in an unknown tongue*
*speaketh not unto men, but unto God: for no*

*man understandeth him; howbeit in the spirit he speaketh mysteries.* (1 Corinthians 14:2)

*Speaking to yourselves in psalms and hymns and spiritual songs, singing and making melody in your heart to the Lord.* (Ephesians 5:19)

Mommy stopped her singing and dancing. She kneeled down upon the soft, green grass and took my face gently in her hands. Mommy looked deep into my eyes with so much love. I love my Mommy so very much. I put my arms around her neck and hugged her tight.

*A new commandment I give unto you, that ye love one another; as I have loved you, that ye also love one another.* (John 13:34) *Beloved, let us love one another, for love is of God; and every one that loveth is born of God and knoweth God. No man hath seen God at any time. If we love one another, God dwelleth in us, and his love is perfected in us.* (1 John 4:7,12)

She said, "My beloved daughter, I sing praises to our Father in Heaven, and Jesus, with the help of the Holy Spirit. I am thanking them for all they are and do for us."

*Enter into his gates with thanksgiving, and into his courts with praise: be thankful unto him, and bless his name.* (Psalms 100:4)

"It is the Holy Spirit that sings through Mommy," she said. "The Holy Spirit will speak and sing through you too, my little one. Ask Him with all your heart and truly mean it, and He will do it."

> *Then Peter said unto them, repent, and be baptized every one of you in the name of Jesus Christ for the remission of sins, and ye shall receive the gift of the Holy Spirit.* (Acts 2:38)

"My precious, little jewel, just like there are many different countries with people who speak many different languages, Mommy praises God in many languages with the help of the Holy Spirit. One language is not enough to give Him all the thanks and glory He deserves."

> *After this I beheld, and lo, a great multitude, which no man could number, of all nations, and kindreds, and people, and tongues, stood before the throne, and before the Lamb, clothed with white robes, and palms in their hands; and cried with a loud voice, saying, Salvation to our God which sitteth upon the throne, and unto the Lamb...Saying, Amen: Blessing, and glory, and wisdom, and thanksgiving, and honor, and power, and might, be unto our God for ever and ever. Amen.* (Revelation 7:9, 12)

Mommy smiled, stood up, and started to sing and dance once again. She sang and danced for Them. I see Jesus in Mommy and Daddy every day. I believed what she said. Like Mommy, I raised my arms high to Heaven and danced. I said, "Holy Spirit, me too!"

> *Ye are our epistle written in or hearts, known and read of all men:* (2 Corinthians 3:2)

*Jesus said unto him, If thou canst believe, all things are possible to him that believeth.* (Mark 9:23)

*And the Holy Spirit descended in a bodily shape like a dove upon him, and a voice came from heaven, which said, thou art my beloved Son; in thee I am well pleased.* (Luke 3:22)

*And when he had said this, he breathed on them, and saith unto them, receive ye the Holy Spirit.* (1 John 20:22)

I opened my mouth and words came tumbling out. My ears heard the new sounds of languages I did not speak before. A soft wind as I spoke continued to flow from my mouth. My heart filled with buckets of love and joy. Pretty songs I sang as I danced just like Mommy.

*And said unto him, Hearest thou what these say? And Jesus saith unto them, yea, have ye never read, out of the mouth of babes and sucklings thou hast perfected praise.* (Matthew 21:15-16)

*And it shall come to pass afterward, that I will pour out my spirit upon all flesh; and your sons and your daughters shall prophesy, your old men shall dream dreams, your young men shall see visions: And also upon the servants and upon the handmaids in those days will I pour out my spirit.* (Joel 2:28-29)

When I opened my eyes, I saw Jesus and His angels dancing with us in the garden! They played their beautiful musical instruments and sounds came from everywhere.

Mommy once told me that our garden could change into a beautiful church without walls. Its colorful, sweet-smelling flowers would fill the air and decorate it too. Its soft, green grass would become a carpet to walk upon, with the yellow sunshine warm and bright. The birds and wind would sing and music would be heard. I giggled joyfully as I watched it happen right before my eyes. My nose filled with sweet-smelling perfumes, and music notes floated in the air as I danced and sang like Mommy. My afternoon was full of Heaven on earth. It was the best 'play date' I ever had. Lots of friends from above visited and filled the garden. It was fun!

> *Praise ye him, all his angels: praise ye him, all his hosts.* (Psalms 148:2)

> *The Lord thy God in the midst of thee is mighty; he will save, he will rejoice over thee with joy; he will rest in his love, he will joy over thee with singing.* (Zephaniah 3:17)

I stopped dancing and singing. I started to yawn. I was sleepy. I cried a little. I wasn't sad or afraid. Something new and wonderful happened to me. I knew because goosebumps were all over me. Lots of fun and new surprises made me breathe much more than before. I changed just like a caterpillar does when it changes into a butterfly. I looked the same and not like a butterfly, but I knew something happy happened to me. I was sure the caterpillar knew it changed inside and out too. A butterfly is different than a caterpillar, so much more than ever before. I wanted much more too. I felt safe and warm all over. Love hugged me, and I hugged it back.

When I looked up, Mommy stood right in front of me. As she reached downward with her arms to hug me, I jumped up and wobbled. Mommy caught me and we both tumbled to the ground. Mommy laughed and I laughed with her. The green grass was like a soft carpet. We sat up and Mommy put her arms around me. I rested in her arms as she rocked me back and forth, humming so sweetly. There was a mother songbird near us. She cried out a warning, protecting her nest of eggs.

As my eyes closed for my afternoon nap, I heard Mommy thanking our Father in Heaven for the beautiful and blessed afternoon, again and again. I thought I heard her crying softly, as I fell asleep in her arms in the garden.

After we ate dinner, Daddy and Mommy helped me understand more about the Holy Spirit. We read several Bible sentences together. I learned that the Holy Spirit is a person like God the Father and Jesus. We were made to look like them and act like them. The Holy Spirit is holy, and not to be forgotten or mistreated. I decided that night to always remember Him and to be kind to Him too.

Before bedtime, Mommy surprised me with the biggest bubble bath ever! It had lots of bubbles and suds. I climbed in and hid in the bubbles, right in front of her.

Mommy said, "I see you!" I jumped up and giggled with joy.

As Mommy scrubbed me squeaky clean with soft soap, I asked her, "Mommy, what is holy?"

> *But who may abide the day of his coming? And who shall stand when he appeareth? for he is like a refiner's fire, and like fullers' soap: And he shall sit as a refiner and purifier of silver: and he shall purify the sons of Levi, and purge them as gold and silver, that they may offer unto the Lord an offering in righteousness.* (Malachi 3:2–3)

She said, "Holy means to be clean inside and outside as we listen to Jesus every day, and really want to obey Him."

She told me it was something like my bubble bath. Mommy said the Holy Spirit makes us clean inside by helping us think good thoughts. He helps us to be clean outside by helping us to do good things. I like to think good thoughts and to do good things. I want to be clean inside and outside. Don't you?

"Mommy," I shouted. "The Holy Spirit is a nice person to help us behave and be like Him. I do like Him!" Mommy smiled and finished my bath. She softly sang one of my favorite songs, the "Three Little Fishies." (1.)

After my bath, Mommy helped me put on my clean pajamas. I smelled like roses. I giggled as I tried to imagine a giant Holy Spirit bubble bath.

# Chapter 6

## Seaside Adventures

Today, Daddy and Mommy and I are going to the seashore. As soon as we arrived at the beach, Mommy put protective sunscreen all over my arms, legs, and face.

"It will keep your skin from burning and turning bright red," Mommy said. It smelled like flowers. I got impatient and wanted her to hurry.

She said, "Just a little more, be still." I waited.

As soon as Mommy was finished, I ran across the warm, soft sand to put my feet into the salt water. Daddy followed me.

Mommy and Daddy swam close beside me. They taught me how to swim and float. Daddy put a lifejacket on me. It covered my green, ruffled bathing suit. It was comfy and colorful. I did learn quickly. A little while later, I could float by myself!

I liked the cool, salty water. The waves played around me. Sometimes, the waves got too big and water got in my mouth. It tasted very salty! I tried not to swallow the salty water. Mommy said, "The creation rejoices in its Creator; that's why the waves are so playful today."

*Let the heavens rejoice, and let the earth be glad; let the sea roar, and the fullness thereof...Before the Lord: for he cometh, for he cometh to judge the earth: he shall judge the world with righteousness, and the people with his truth.* (Psalm 96:11-13)

*Let the heaven and the earth praise him, the seas, and everything that moveth therein.* (Psalm 69:34)

*The floods have lifted up, O Lord, the floods have lifted up their voice; the floods lift up their waves.* (Psalm 93:3)

Later on, we searched for treasures from the sea along the sandy seashore. Together, we found seashells and colorful seaweed.

"Seaweed comes from the gardens in the sea and oceans. A food from Heaven with lots of minerals," Mommy said. "Just like we have a garden, the sea is full of gardens."

I put the pretty-colored seaweed in my blue bucket. They felt rubbery. Some were flat and some had round pods on them. I carried my prize with great joy!

> *Now therefore, if ye will obey my voice indeed,*
> *and keep my covenant, then ye shall be a peculiar*
> *treasure unto me above all people: for all the earth*
> *is mine.* (Exodus 19:5)

Before it was time to go, I found a big shell close by that was white with brown ridges and whorls. It looked like a Dairy Queen ice cream.

"Mommy! Daddy!" I yelled, excited. "Look, look what I found!"

Daddy smiled and said, "Wow, what a treasure you found. That's a whelk, hard to find."

I was so pleased with my discovery, a rare shell to find. Daddy said that I should always remember to thank God for His beautiful work, for He made the shell and gave it to me. I did remember to thank Him.

> *Train up a child in the way he should go, and when*
> *he is old, he will not depart from it.* (Proverbs 22:6)

> *The heavens are thine, the earth also is thine: as*
> *for the world and the fullness thereof, thou hast*
> *founded them.* (Psalm 89:11)

When it was time to go, I held onto Mommy and Daddy's hand as we walked off the beach. Mommy said, "God made everything beautiful in His time."

As I listened to Mommy speak, I looked up at the sky and watched the sun slowly disappear. Orange and gold colored the sky. My mouth dropped open wide. It was the colors of my chalk at home! God must be an artist too. His canvas is the big sky, and the earth gives the colors to paint with, up and down.

*The heavens declare the glory of God; and the*
*firmament showeth his handiwork. Day after day*
*uttereth speech, and night unto night sheweth*

*knowledge. There is no speech nor language, where their voice is not heard. Their line is gone out through all the earth, and their words to the end of the world. In them hath he set a tabernacle for the sun. This is as a bridegroom coming out of his chamber, and rejoiceth as a strong man to run a race. His going forth is from the end of the heaven, and his circuit unto the ends of it: and there is nothing hid from the heat thereof.* (Psalms 19:1-6)

Before I go to sleep at night, Daddy always finds time to read to me. We have many books filled with pictures of trees, planets, animals, fish, musical instruments, and butterflies. My favorite stories are stories from the Bible. I ask Daddy to read them to me over and over again. He does, because he likes them too. Each time is like the first time when we read it.

*Therefore shall ye lay up these my words in your heart and in your soul, and bind them for a sign upon your hand, that they may be as frontlets between your eyes. And ye shall teach them your children, speaking of them when thou sittest in thine house, and when thou walkest by the way, when thou liest down, and when thou risest up.* (Deuteronomy 11:18-19)

Every time Daddy reads a story, I understand something new. I am sure Daddy does too. Sometimes, he stops reading, and his eyes light up like lightbulbs. That is why he reads them again to find another treasure. It makes me feel good inside when he reads them to me. I hope Daddy feels the same as me.

*And there are also many other things which Jesus did, the which, if they should be written every one, I suppose that even the world itself could not contain the books that should be written. Amen.* (John 21:25)

I ask Daddy so many questions. He never gets tired of answering them. Sometimes, he asks me questions.

Daddy said that God made the earth, the stars, the trees, the creatures, and me. He said that God knew me even before I was born! How could that be?

*For thou hast possessed my reins: thou hast covered me in my mother's womb. I will praise thee; for I am fearfully and wonderfully made: marvelous are thy works; and that my soul knoweth right well. My substance was not hid from thee, when I was made in secret, and curiously wrought in the lowest parts of the earth. Thine eyes did see my substance, yet being unperfect; and in thy book all my members were written, which in continuance were fashioned, when as yet there was none of them.* (Psalms 139:13-16)

# Chapter 7

# Music and Prayer

Music has a special place in our home. Mommy plays the harp and Daddy, the trumpet. I like to play the piano.

I have lessons twice a month. I practice on our baby grand piano in the parlor. It was a gift from my grandpa and grandma. Grandpa plays the tuba and grandma, the violin.

Mommy and I play together. Daddy likes to jump in with his trumpet. We have our own little orchestra! Sometimes, I am the conductor. I am a great conductor. My arms wave this way and that way. I don't know for sure if Mommy and Daddy can keep up with me.

We laugh and laugh so much after we play that sometimes tears appear on our faces. Mommy kisses my face over and over again. We have so much fun with music. Gentle, musical sounds fill my heart right up!

> *Praise him with the sound of the trumpet: praise him with the psaltery and harp...praise him with stringed instruments and organs.* (Psalms 150:3,4)

Daddy is funny, but also serious at times. I follow him around the house when he blows his trumpet and shofar in honor of King Jesus.

He says, "Jesus is King of Kings and Lord of Lords!"

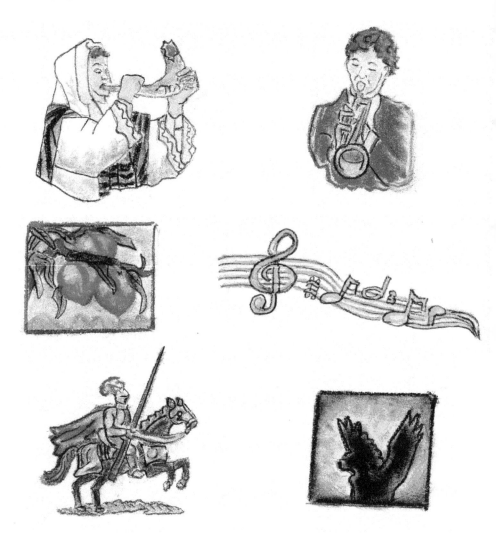

*Praise him with the sound of the trumpet: praise him with the psaltery and harp.* (Psalms 150:3)

*And he hath on his vesture and on his thigh a name written, King of Kings, and Lord of Lords.* (Revelation 19:16)

I know Daddy loves Jesus by the way his heart speaks about Him. Daddy said, "Words come from people's hearts. What is in their hearts come out of their mouth. God looks at the heart."

> *But the Lord said unto Samuel, look not on his countenance, or on the height of his stature; because I have refused him: for the Lord seeth not as a man seeth; for man looketh on the outward appearance, but the Lord looketh on the heart.* (1 Samuel 16:7)

> *A good man out of the good treasure of his heart bringeth forth that which is good; and an evil man out of the evil treasure of his heart bringeth forth that which is evil: for of the abundance of the heart his mouth speaketh.* (Luke 6:45)

Daddy pointed to a peach tree once and said, "Now, that's a peach tree!"

He said, "You know what kind of tree it is by its fruit. It is the same way with people."

> *He shall know them by their fruit. Do men gather grapes of thorns, or figs of thistles? Even so every good tree bringeth forth good fruit; but a corrupt tree bringeth forth evil fruit. A good tree cannot bring forth evil fruit, neither can a corrupt tree bring forth good fruit.* (Matthew 7:15-20)

> *Either make the tree good, and his fruit good; or else make the tree corrupt, and his fruit corrupt: for the tree is known by his fruit.* (Matthew 12:33)

I couldn't imagine an apple tree with thistles growing on it instead of apples. Could you? Shouldn't an apple tree have apples on it? How can an apple tree make others believe it is an apple tree when it isn't ? You really have to look at its fruit first to know what kind of tree it is. I will have to look closely, for thistles hurt.

Sounds of Heavenly music floats throughout our house. Mommy said harmony and peace live in our house. We welcome them. I know peace and I know harmony. They help me think beautiful thoughts.

> *And the fruit of righteousness is sown in peace of them that make peace.* (James 3:18)

> *And the peace of God, which passeth all understanding, shall keep your hearts and minds through Christ Jesus. Finally, brethren, whatsoever things are true, whatsoever things are honest, whatsoever things are just, whatsoever things are pure, whatsoever things are lovely, whatsoever things are of good report; if there be any virtue, and if there be any praise, think on these things.* (Philippians 4:7-8)

When Mommy plays the harp, little ripples from its strings run through my body. The sounds make me feel peaceful. They reach inside my heart. I become sleepy as I lie against Mommy's chest, with my arms wrapped gently around her neck. Soon, I fall asleep upon her lap as she continues to practice her harp music.

> *Praise the Lord with the harp: sing unto him with the psaltery and an instrument of ten strings.* (Psalms 32:2)

44

One night, I jumped out of bed and ran to Daddy and Mommy's bedroom. I wasn't very sleepy. Mommy and Daddy were praying. They were not sleepy, either! I listened as they prayed.

*But thou, when thou prayest, enter into thy closet, and when thou hast shut thy door, pray to thy Father which is in secret; and thy Father which seeth in secret shall reward thee openly.* (Matthew 6:6)

Daddy asked Jesus to watch over us and keep us safe. He prayed for Mommy, Grandpa, Grandma and me. Daddy prayed for other families too.

Daddy kept praying. Whatever he prayed, I prayed too. It didn't matter if the words were too big for me to say or understand. I knew it was important and the right thing to do. He prayed for our city and our country. He prayed for the peace of Jerusalem. Daddy shouted, "God bless the USA!"

*Pray without ceasing.* (1 Thessalonians 5:17)

*Pray for the peace of Jerusalem: they shall prosper that love thee.* (Psalms 122:6)

*If my people, which are called by my name, shall humble themselves, and pray, and seek my face, and turn from their wicked ways; then I will hear from heaven, and will heal their land.* (2 Chronicles 7:14)

Daddy prayed for the government, for the schools, for the military, for the policemen and women, for the president, for the churches, for the music and the movies, for the economy, and for education. He prayed and prayed. He sent righteousness and holiness upon the news that they would only tell people the truth.

*I exhort therefore, that, first of all, supplications, prayers, intercessions, and giving of thanks, be made for all men; For kings, and for all that are in authority; that we may lead a quiet and peaceable life in all godliness and honesty. For this is good and acceptable in the sight of God our Savior.* (1 Timothy 2:1-3)

When we finished praying, Mommy thanked Jesus for listening and answering our prayers in His time and way.

She said, "Glory to you, my Father! Your kingdom come and Your will be done on earth as it is in Heaven."

> *The effectual fervent prayer of a righteous man avails much.* (James 5:16)

> *If ye abide in me, and my words abide in you, ye shall ask what ye will and it shall be done unto you.* (John 15:7)

I know Daddy prays for me every night. When he thinks I am fast asleep, he tip-toes into my bedroom and prays. I smile because Daddy sounds like a soldier battling the darkness.

*Finally my brethren, be strong in the Lord, and in the power of his might. Put on the whole armour of God that ye may be able to stand against the wiles of the devil. For we wrestle not against flesh and blood, but against principalities, against powers, against the rulers of the darkness of this world, against spiritual wickedness in high places.*
(Ephesians 6:10-18)

*And I will give unto thee the keys of the kingdom of heaven: and whatsoever thou shalt bind on earth shall be bound in heaven: and whatsoever thou shalt loose on earth shall be loosed in heaven.*
(Matthew 16:19)

Daddy shouted, "The blood of Jesus paid it all! It is done; it is finished! We stand in that victory. The battle is the Lord's. He is the King. He rules and reigns and we rule and reign with Him. We have all power and authority over the darkness!"

My eyes got heavy and closed. I was so comfy and warm on the bed. I felt safe and happy. I fell fast asleep, while Daddy and Mommy continued to pray.

# Chapter 8

# Dinner and King Solomon

Dinner is one of my favorite meals. I also like breakfast. I get to help Mommy bake bread and set the table. We have so much fun in the kitchen. Sometimes, when the flour gets on my face Mommy kisses my nose.

> *Go thy way, eat thy bread with joy, and drink thy wine with a merry heart; for God now accepteth thy works.* (Ecclesiastics 9:7)

> *Give us this day our daily bread.* (Matthew 6:11)

I help Mommy put pretty plates with pictures of fish, birds, and seashells on the dining room table. It is called "setting the table."

The flowers we picked from our garden in the morning sat in a glass vase in the middle of the table. Mommy enjoys having lots of flowers in the house, especially during the summer. They smell nice and look so pretty too.

> *I am the rose of Sharon, and the lily of the valleys.*
> (Song of Solomon 2:11)

> *Then took Mary a pound of ointment of spikenard, very costly, and anointed the feet of Jesus, and wiped his feet with her hair: and the house was filled with the odour of the ointment.* (John 12:3)

Mommy cooked the vegetables and herbs we picked from our garden today. Fresh vegetables are tasty and good for me. She cooked Daddy's favorite dish, lamb stew with vegetables.

Daddy will be happy! He works like the bees in their hives. He gives lots of attention to his work. Daddy helps people in his work too.

> *And behold, I come quickly; and my reward is with me, to give every man according as his work shall be.* (Revelation 22:12)

> *But let every man prove his own work, and then shall he have rejoicing in himself alone, and not another.* (Galatians 6:4)

Mommy loves Daddy and he loves Mommy. They love me too. Mommy is a good Mommy. She takes care of us. She listens to Daddy, and together they have lots of fun.

> *A new commandment I give unto you, that ye love one another; as I have loved you, that ye also love one another. By this shall all men know that ye are my disciples, if ye love one another.* (John 13:34-35)

> *Who can find a virtuous woman? For her price is far above rubies The heart of her husband doth safely trust in her, so that he shall have no need of spoil. She will do him good and not evil all the days of her life. She seeketh wool, and flax, and worketh willingly with her hands. She is like a merchants' ship; she bringeth forth her food from afar. She riseth also while it is yet night, and giveth meat to her household and a portion to her maidens.* (Proverbs 31:10-31)

*Wives, submit yourselves unto your own husbands,
as unto the Lord...Husbands, love your wives, even
as Christ also loved the church, and gave himself
for it.* (Ephesians 5:22-32)

For dessert, Mommy made a berry pie. I helped cut berries and leaves out of the dough for the crust.

I get hungry fast, but before we eat, Daddy prays and asks Jesus to bless our bread and water, and the air we breathe. This keeps sickness from us and the food tastes better! Daddy and Mommy are thankful for all God's blessings, and so am I. Aren't you?

*And ye shall serve the Lord your God, and he
shall bless thy bread, and thy water; and I
will take sickness away from the midst of thee.*
(Exodus 23:25)

*For every creature of God is good, and nothing
to be refused, if it be received with thanksgiving:
For it is sanctified by the word of God and prayer.*
(1 Timothy 4:4-5)

I helped Mommy put different flowers in vases throughout the house. We put together flowers by their colors and shapes. We sometimes place them by the way they smell. When we finished, Mommy smiled and said, "You are quite the little florist!" This made me feel loved.

I remembered one morning when we went flower picking in our garden, Mommy reminded me about the story of King Solomon.

He was the wisest and richest of kings, and had such colorful clothes. Mommy pointed to one of the flowers I held in my hands.

She said, "God's word from the Bible says that all of King Solomon's beautiful clothes could not be compared to the beauty and fashion of one little flower that God made."

*And why take ye thought for raiment? Consider the lilies of the field, how they grow; they toil not, neither do they spin: And yet I say unto you, That even Solomon in all his glory was not arrayed like one of these.* (Matthew 6:28-29)

I was surprised at what Mommy told me. I looked at the flower for a long time, and then at my pretty, garden-print, chiffon-laced dress. I touched my dress with my fingertips and slowly touched the flower's petals. I wanted to find out which one was the prettiest and softest, my dress or the flower. The flower was much softer than my dress and it was alive. The colorful petals around it were dressed by God, but my dress was made by someone who sewed it. King Solomon's clothes were not made like the flower either. They were made by people. The flower truly is the winner because the flower and its dress were made by God. My heart pictured what Mommy meant and I quickly understood. What do you think? Which one is the winner?

# Chapter 9

# Whales and Jonah

My first whale watch was a surprise. Early one morning, Daddy said, "Today, little one, you will see the whales!"

*And God created great whales, and every living creature that moveth, which the waters brought forth abundantly, after their kind, and every winged fowl after his kind: and God saw that it was good.* (Genesis 1:21)

I knew what whales looked like from the pictures and stories we read, but I never saw a real one up close. Mommy taught me about the different kinds of whales and played some of their songs for me, but today Daddy said I would see them! I trusted Daddy. He always kept his promises. Whenever something happened that we couldn't go on the time we planned, we made sure we went another time. It always worked out, sometimes even better!

Off we went and got on a boat. It was a big boat! Much bigger than me.

Mommy bundled me up for the ride, for it took some time to get to where the whales fed. Mommy shared that long ago there were so many whales that all one had to do was look at them from the seashore. But now, there were only so few left. I asked Mommy why that was so, and she told me. She said, "Many were hunted for their oil, blubber, and bones almost to extinction." I felt sad. I knew what extinction meant. It is a species that no longer exists. A species is a group of living creatures that are the same. I asked Jesus to help them.

"Jesus," I prayed. "Please make more whales and protect those that are still here. I am sorry we hurt them. Thank you."

*And Jesus said unto them, Because of your unbelief: for verily I say unto you, If ye have faith as a grain of mustard seed, ye shall say unto this mountain, remove hence to yonder place; and it shall remove; and nothing shall be impossible unto you.* (Matthew 17:20)

The boat went out across the sea slowly. It was windy and the waves hit against the sides of the boat. My hat stayed on my head. Mommy tied it gently under my chin. I was warm and felt adventurous, just like a sea captain!

Inside the cabin, a girl showed us pictures of the Humpback whales. They all had names! I wondered if the whale that swallowed Jonah had a name. I asked her if she knew the story about Jonah and the whale. She did not know it, and asked me to tell her about it. I did and she liked it.

*Now the Lord had prepared a great fish to swallow up Jonah. And Jonah was in the belly of the fish three days and three nights.* (Jonah 1:17)

I asked, "Will we see the whale that swallowed Jonah today?" The girl answered, "Maybe!"

This made me so happy! I asked, "Do you know its name too?" She answered, "No, I don't think he or she was ever given a name."

The boat finally slowed to a stop. We saw whales close by and far away. Some surfaced near the boat for air, but quickly dove under.

"Mommy!" I yelled. "Look, there is one!"

We kept moving back and forth across the boat to see them. A voice from the loud speaker shouted, "Whale at one o'clock, and one at nine o'clock."

Daddy went one way and we went the other. We laughed when we bumped into each other.

> *A merry heart doeth good like a medicine; but a*
> *broken spirit drieth the bones.* (Proverbs 17:22)

The whales were almost as big as the boat. They swam close but didn't bump into us. I was not afraid. The whales would not hurt us. Their tails were so big! They splashed, and down they went! I watched them disappear again and again.

A small, black head surfaced, with bubbles all around it, right in front of us. Its eyes watched us . It was as if it knew us.

I cried out, "Hello! Hello! What is your name? Do you have a Mommy and Daddy too?"

It dove down into the sea. It stayed under for a very long time. The next time I saw it, it was far away.

"Daddy!" I shouted. "How can they hold their breath so long? Why can't I hold my breath under water like they do?"

Daddy explained, "Every creature that our Heavenly Father created is unique, perfectly made to exist in their given surroundings. Whales live in the seas and oceans. The whales need to be able to swim far beneath the water to eat. They must hold their breath for a long time before they can come back up to the top to breathe."

Mommy added, "Humpback whales sing beautiful songs to their Creator and each other. They bless the seas and oceans with praises to God, the Almighty. They were made for our enjoyment too."

> *O Lord, how manifold are thy works! In wisdom hast thou made them all: the earth is full of thy riches, so is this great and wide sea, wherein are things creeping innumerable, both small and great beasts.* (Psalms 104:24-25)

> *Praise ye him, sun and moon: praise him, all ye stars of light... Praise the Lord from the earth, ye dragons, and all deeps:...Let them praise the name of the Lord: for he commanded and they were created.* (Psalms 148: 1-14)

Mommy said that soon the whales would sing a new song of redemption, for the sons and daughters of glory were being shown. Before I could ask what she meant, Mommy answered, with such joy: "We are the daughters of glory, sleeping beauties who are finally waking up and listening to Him! The whales will share in our freedom from harm and being hunted. You, my little one, will understand more about what I say in the time to come."

*For it became him, for whom are all things, and by whom are all things, in bringing many sons unto glory, to make the captain of their salvation perfect through sufferings.* (Hebrews 2:10)

*For the earnest expectation of the creature waiteth for the manifestation of the sons of God.* (Romans 8:19-23)

I clapped my hands, closed my eyes, and thought about sleeping beauty waking up after such a long time. I was so excited for her and us! Waking up like sleeping beauty is a wonderful thing!

*Wherefore he saith, Awake thou that sleepest, and arise from the dead, and Christ shall give thee light.* (Ephesians 5:14)

*And that, knowing the time, that now it is high time to awake out of sleep: for now is our salvation nearer than when we believed.* (Romans 13:11)

Daddy taught me a little about Heaven's culture. He said, "When we listen, obey, and live for Jesus, our prayers and choices heal the earth and above. The sky, the planets, the seas, the land, the creatures, the fish, the plants, and the waters wait for us to do it."

"We have the authority and power to govern time, space, and the creation. We just don't use it," Daddy said.

"Daddy, what does 'govern' mean? I asked. He gave me examples to understand the word govern. First he told me that our prayers are powerful, to govern by prayer. For the whales, we can send out the Hosts from Heaven to stop the whalers from hunting them by disarming their harpoons. We can ask God in Jesus's Name to heal the rivers and seas and pray that His will be done to bring heaven on earth.

> *For the creature was made subject to vanity, not willingly, but by reason of him who hath subjected the same in hope. Because the creature itself shall be delivered from the bondage of corruption into the glorious liberty of the children of God.* (Romans 8:20)

Daddy looked at me very seriously when I asked him if the earth was sick and he answered, "Yes, the earth is sick right now, but soon it will be healed and made better."

Daddy shared that since we were made from the earth like the rest of all creation, we shared a common bond with it. They suffered too because of our disobedience. But, God out of love for us kept us first, and above all else, and He let them also be included in His plan for healing. The creation would share in the beautiful wholeness with us.

> *And the Lord God formed man of the dust of the ground, and breathed into his nostrils the breath of life; and man became a living soul. And the Lord God planted a garden eastward in Eden: and there he put the man whom he formed.* (Genesis 2:7-8)

Daddy said, "Our Father in Heaven breathed His breath of life into us and gave life to all. It is important for us to take care of ourselves and the earth."

> I prayed, "Jesus, please heal the earth! I promise to take care of it and pray for it too. I will try hard

to obey Mommy and Daddy. I will listen to them just like they do to You, because I love them." I feel so good when I obey Mommy and Daddy! Don't you?

# Chapter 10

# Horse Polo and Trophies

Daddy plays horse polo. He enjoys this sport very much. Sometimes, he is invited to practice and play in tournaments nearby. His friends have several fine polo horses that he can ride.

*Be kindly affectioned one to another with brotherly love; in honour preferring one another.* (Romans 12:10)

*And to godliness brotherly kindness; and to brotherly kindness charity.* (2 Peter 1:7)

Sometimes Mommy and I watch Daddy practice. We set up a table behind our Land Rover when there is a tournament and have a picnic. Picnics are fun! Mommy packs fruits and cheeses in a brown basket. I eat some of each. The cheese is always yummy!

I like the horses very much. I enjoy watching them run back and forth to make a goal. They chase a small ball. I have fun when we run out to the field in between games and stomp on the grass to fit it back into the ground. The horses' legs and muscles are magnificent to watch when they run. How strong they are and how fast they go! When they run, I remember the story of Job in the Bible, and how the horse runs straight into the battle and is not afraid.

> *Hast thou given the horse strength? Hast thou clothed his neck with thunder? Canst thou make him afraid as a grasshopper? The glory of his nostrils is terrible. He paweth in the valley, and rejoiceth in his strength: he goeth on to meet the armed men. He mocketh at fear, and he is not affrighted; neither turneth he back from the sword. The quiver rattleth against him, the glittering spear and the shield. He swalloweth the ground with fierceness and rage: neither believeth he that it is the sound of the trumpet. He saith among the trumpets, Ha, ha; and smelleth the battle afar off, the thunder of the captains, and the shouting. (Job 39:19-25)*

Maybe when I get bigger like Daddy, I could play horse polo too!

> *Delight thyself also in the Lord; and he shall give thee the desires of thine heart. (Psalms 37:4)*

Daddy is kind to his friends' horses whenever he practices or plays. I watch Daddy. He respects God's creation.

*A righteous man regardeth the life of his beast: but the tender mercies of the wicked are cruel.* (Proverbs 12:10)

*Put on therefore, as the elect of God, holy and beloved, bowels of mercies, kindness, humbleness of mind, meekness, long suffering.* (Colossians 3:12)

He taught me to respect the creation. Daddy never hurts any creature. He rescues them! He said, "My little love, never hurt any creature for they cry too, and God sees all."

*Train up a child in the way he should go: and when he is old, he will not depart from it.* (Proverbs 22:6)

We have two Scottish Deerhounds that Daddy rescued. They love and protect us. They even watch over our chickens.

Mommy and I run out to greet Daddy in the field when he finishes playing. Daddy kisses Mommy as he picks her up in his arms, and twirls her around before he lets her down.

*A new commandment I give unto you, That ye love one another; as I have loved you, that ye also love one another.* (John 13:34)

Daddy did the same with me. He picked me up, twirled me around, and kissed my head. I giggled and giggled. Daddy always said that when he helped the team win a game, it was like he was running the race to obtain the prize of the high call in Christ, Jesus.

*I press toward the mark for the prize of the high calling of God in Christ Jesus.* (Philippians 3:14)

*Wherefore, seeing we also are compassed about with so great a cloud of witnesses, let us lay aside every weight, and the sin which doth so easily beset us, and let us run with patience the race that is set before us, Looking unto Jesus the author and finisher of our faith; who for the joy that was set before him endured the cross, despising the shame, and is set down at the right hand of the throne of God.* (Hebrews 12:1-2)

"This is the truest trophy of all!" Daddy said. "The high call of God in Christ, Jesus!"

I hope to win this trophy one day! Don't you?

# Discussion/Guidance Questions

1. Does Jesus have a house too? Where is Jesus's house?

2. Are honeybees special? What can they do?

3. Would you like to sing and dance with the Holy Spirit too?

4. What is your favorite bible story?

5. Do you play a musical instrument? Which one?

6. Are you an artist too? Do you like to draw?

7. Have you planted a garden yet? Which vegetable is your favorite?

8. Which one dresses the best, a flower or King Solomon?

9. Whale Watches are fun! Have you been on one yet?

10. A telescope helps you see the planets and stars above. Have you looked through one yet?

# Bibliography

1.  Kyser, Kay. Song: "The Three Little Fishies." 1939. ("Holy Spirit, Me Too!") Chap. 5, page 37. https://youtu.be/-963CTDLy68

*Lyrics*

Down in the meadow in the ittie bitty pool
Swam the three little fishies and a mama fishie too
"Swim" said the mama fishie, "Swim if you can"
And they swam, swam, swam right over the dam

Down in the meadow in the ittie bitty pool
Swam three little fishies and a mama fishie too
"Swim" said the mama fishie, "Swim if you can"
And they swam and they swam right over the dam

Boop boop dittem dattem wattem chu
Boop boop dittem dattem wattem chu
Boop boop dittem dattem wattem chu

And they swam and they swam all over the dam
"Stop" said the mama fishie, "Or you will get lost"
But the three little fishies didn't wanna be bossed
So the three little fishies went off on a spree
And they swam, swam, swam right out to the sea

"Stop" said the mama fishie, "You'll get lost"
But the three little fishies didn't wanna be bossed
The three little fishies went out on a spree
And they swam and they swam right out to the sea

Boop boop riddle diddle razzle brrrp
Boop boop riddle diddle razzle brrrp
Boop boop riddle diddle razzle brrrp

"Whee" yelled the fishies, "Oh, here's a lot of fun
Swim in the sea 'til the day is done"
So they swam and they swam, it was all a lark

'Til all of a sudden they met a shark
"Whee" yelled the little fishies, "Lots of fun
We'll swim in the sea 'til the day is done"
And they swam and they swam and it was a lark
'Til all of a sudden they saw a shark

Boop boop skiddly-did
Boop boop skiddly-did
Boop boop skiddly-did

"Help" cried the fishies, "Oh, look at the whales"
Quick as they could, they turned on their tails
Back to the pool in the meadow they swam
And swam and they swam back over the dam

"Help" cried the little fishies, "Look at the whales"
Quick as they could, they turned on their tails
And back to the pool in the meadow they swam
And they swam and they swam back over the dam

Boop boop foo, foodly racky sacky
Boop boop foo, foodly racky sacky
Boop boop foo

And they swam and swam back over the dam
Oh, that shark almost ate us
For seafood, mama

CPSIA information can be obtained
at www.ICGtesting.com
Printed in the USA
LVHW071643151121
703397LV00021B/615

9 781662 831287